About the Author

I was born in a rough and tough area of west London, but spent my first years in Germany where I was inspired by the Brothers Grimm fairy tales and German folklore. My love for these mystical tales that have hidden moral lessons sparked my passion for art and creativity. Several years later, my family moved backed to London and then eventually settled on the south coast of Dorset. It is here on the south coast by the sea that I met my husband, had my children and decided to follow my dreams by studying illustration and design which eventually lead me to composing and illustrating my own stories based on the essence of my inspirations.

MAGIC WAND TALES

Donna Mintey

Magic Wand Tales

Olympia Publishers
London

www.olympiapublishers.com
OLYMPIA PAPERBACK EDITION

A CIP catalogue record for this title is
available from the British Library.

ISBN: 978-1-78830-452-8

First Published in 2019

Olympia Publishers
60 Cannon Street
London
EC4N 6NP

Printed in Great Britain

ERIS CASTLE
HOME OF THE GREAT WIZARD
CRESENT MOON COTTAGE
HOME OF THE WITCH'S CAT
NEW MOON COTTAGE
HOME OF CAT'S FRIEND
BLUE MOON COTTAGE
HOME OF THE WICKED FAIRY
HARVEST MOON MANNER
HOME OF THE BIGGEST BAD CAT IN TOWN
RUMBLE MOUNTAINS
HOME OF THE TROLLS
N
W
E
S
ERIS CASTLE
LUNA ISLAND
TEARDROP POND

THE MILKY WAY SEA
CRESENT MOON COTTAGE
NEW MOON COTTAGE
SUPERNOVA ISLAND
THE WISHING WELL
RUMBLE MOUNTAINS
BLUE MOON COTTAGE
LOVE LAKE
HARVEST MOON MANNER
WISPER FOREST
RED DWARF COVE

Dedication

With many thanks to my lovely husband, Andy, my children, Amy and Justin and all my grandchildren.

The witch's cat watched as the witch packed her bag. From spell books to potions and a quick kiss goodbye, she jumped on her broomstick and took to the sky. The witch's cat looked and saw that she left the....

Magic Wand

that was still on her desk...

ALOE VERA
healing plant

Mmm… thought the cat, what harm could it do? Just a little play to magic some food. So he grabbed the wand and jiggled about, casting a spell to magic a mouse!

With a FLASH and a BANG
the wand did its stuff,
but instead of a mouse it turned cat to a

FROUSE!

mouse.....
DINNER

DINNER

With BIG pink eyes and STRIPY blue
hair, LONG claws and teeth
the cat despaired.....
“oh no, what have I done?
I’ve gone from a cat and turned into a

mun!”

Try as he might to undo the spell,
he was stuck and he knew that he needed
some help.

He jumped out of the window and to his friend's house, but his friend ran away from the sight of a Frouse. Poor cat tried to speak but the only sound made was more of a squeak!

9
New Moon
COTTAGE

He trundled back to his home, but
soon realised that he wasn't alone.
He heard a noise from the cupboard
under the stairs and a strong smell of
TROLL hang about in the air.
The witch's cat knew that trolls were bad,
as it didn't take much to make one mad!
He begun to tremble from head to toe -

WHAT COULD HE DO TO MAKE THE TROLL GO?!

Trolls like cats, but only to eat. They'd

MUNCH ON HIS
FINGERS AND
NIBBLE HIS FEET!

The poor witch's cat grew even more scared and knew that he needed to

prepare.

Suddenly the noises stopped.
The door swung open
and out the troll
FLOPPED...

COOKIES
GINGER BEER
BISCUI

Big and scary she looked Cat in the eye,
and right at the
moment Cat let out a cry.
But the troll screeched in fear and ran
straight out the house as never before had
she seen a

FROUSE!

The witch's cat sighed with big relief
and pondered how close he had come
to defeat.

"I could of been a troll's dinner today,
but because I'm frouse I scaried it away. "
And whilst he sat there happy to be,
he heard the witch come back from
her spree.

The witch was shocked to see a Frouse, especially one that was sat in her house, then she saw her Magic Wand and realised what the cat had done... "Oh dear Cat, you silly bean..." playing with wands is not the done thing. It takes years of training to cast the right spell and I can tell you many Magic Wand Tales, but I think you have learnt your lesson today and I'm sure a Frouse you don't want to stay."

With a swish of her wand the witch broke the spell and the witch's cat was back to himself.

PUSH CAT
Big Juicey Fish Supper
DINNER

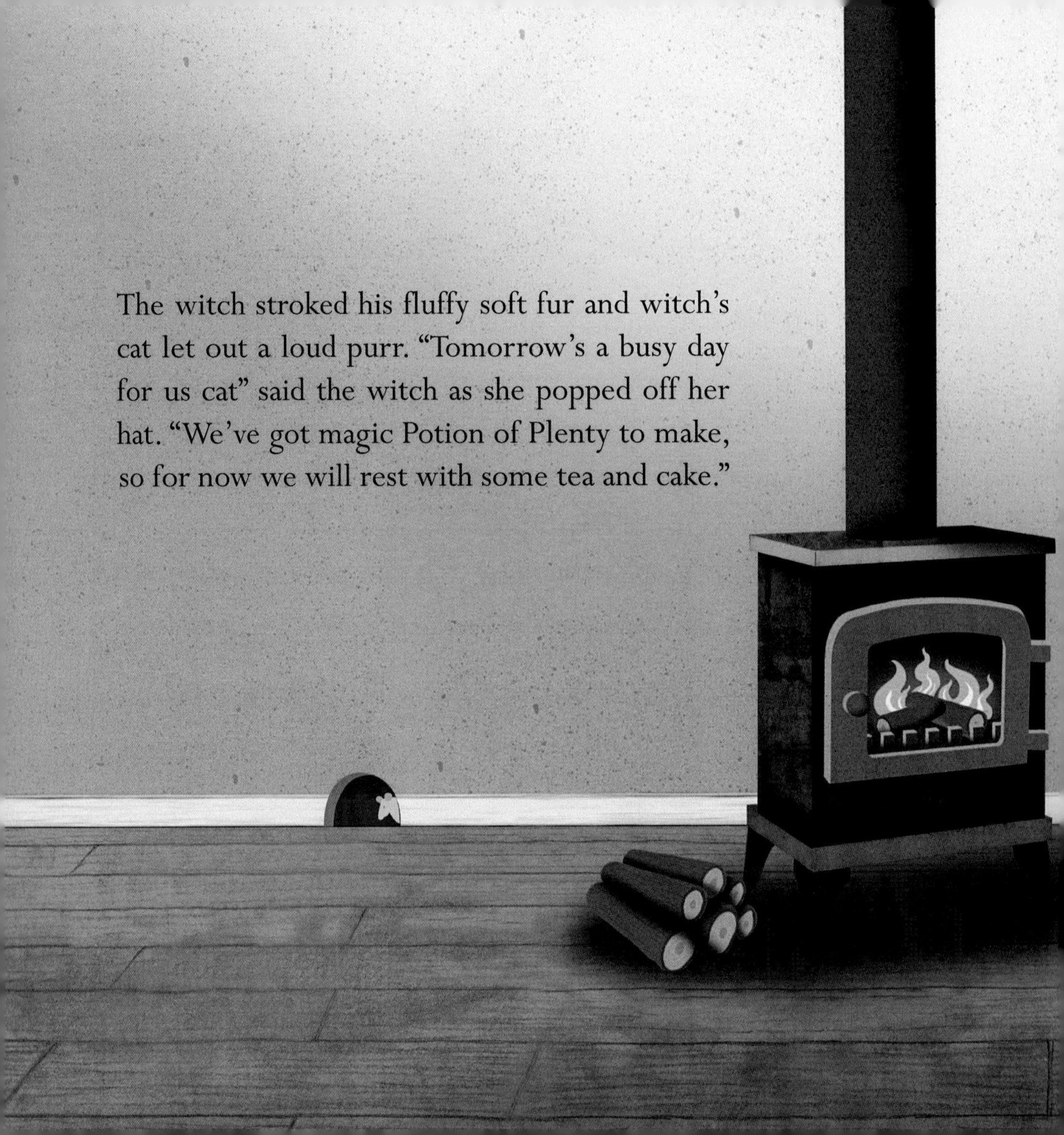

The witch stroked his fluffy soft fur and witch's cat let out a loud purr. "Tomorrow's a busy day for us cat" said the witch as she popped off her hat. "We've got magic Potion of Plenty to make, so for now we will rest with some tea and cake."

MYSTIC
MOMENTS
TREATS

THE END (FOR NOW)